JPIC Ricker
Ricker, Marcella author.
The Sugar Witch switch /

34028087329083
NW $12.45 ocn889329420
04/17/15

3 4028 08732 9083
HARRIS COUNTY PUBLIC LIBRARY

W9-AMO-595

The Sugar Witch Switch

MARCELLA RICKER

Copyright © 2014 Marcella Ricker.

All rights reserved. No part of this book may be used or reproduced by any means, graphic, electronic, or mechanical, including photocopying, recording, taping or by any information storage retrieval system without the written permission of the publisher except in the case of brief quotations embodied in critical articles and reviews.

Archway Publishing books may be ordered through booksellers or by contacting:

Archway Publishing
1663 Liberty Drive
Bloomington, IN 47403
www.archwaypublishing.com
1-(888)-242-5904

Because of the dynamic nature of the Internet, any web addresses or links contained in this book may have changed since publication and may no longer be valid. The views expressed in this work are solely those of the author and do not necessarily reflect the views of the publisher, and the publisher hereby disclaims any responsibility for them.

Certain stock imagery © Thinkstock.
Any people depicted in stock imagery provided by Thinkstock are models, and such images are being used for illustrative purposes only.

ISBN: 978-1-4808-0691-7 (e)
ISBN: 978-1-4808-0692-4 (sc)
ISBN: 978-1-4808-0690-0 (hc)

Printed in the United States of America

Archway Publishing rev. date: 4/17/2014

This book is dedicated to Lily, Holden, and all children who love Halloween.

One warm and windy Halloween night, a very shy, young boy was suiting up in his costume to begin his quest of trick or treating. Holden stepped into his armor and pulled his helmet down over his dark brown eyes. He picked up his feathered lance. He wondered if he would be brave enough to tickle a dragon with it if he ran into one this evening. He grabbed his treat bag and bravely stepped into the darkness.

There were so many giggling children running in the shiny, moonlit street, crossing leaf littered lawns, lining up on pumpkin guarded porches, waiting anxiously for candy to hit the bottom of their bags, that Holden had not noticed the tall figure standing in line behind him.

Holden clanged and clamored his way to the next house and once again the same silent and strange trick or treater moved in quietly behind him in line. So tall and strong, so white and shiny, the shimmering witch must be someone's older sister. Holden counted the children around him and saw Lily, dressed as a purple ninja and Emma, dressed as a cowgirl. Maybe the giant, white witch was with them. Kerplunk! The chocolate bar hit the bottom of Holden's treat bag and he was rattling his way to the next house.

The brave knight crunched along the dry, leafy street, tripping over a twisty twig. Holden tumbled to the ground. As two circus clowns ran by, he searched the fallen leaves for his lance that went flying when he fell. He spotted the lance next to a big, gray boulder in Mr. Sawyer's garden. Perched on the rock, was the oversized, white witch. Long, white fingers grabbed the lance and offered it to Holden.

"Thank you. Why are you sitting here?" Holden asked in a whisper.

"I am trying to get candy and every person in every house I go to, tells me that I am too big to trick or treat." answered the white witch.

"Are you some kind of magic fairy?" asked Holden.

"No, I am the Sugar Witch," laughed the white witch. "I use the candy to build my sugar castle," she added. "Will you give me your candy?" she asked, knowing that Holden wouldn't want to share his candy with a stranger.

Holden clutched his treat bag and his feathery lance. He slowly stepped away as the Sugar Witch stepped behind him. Holden shook nervously as he rang the bell at each house on his street that night, as the Sugar Witch waited. Holden tried to eat as much of his candy as he could, but his head pounded and his stomach ached. The Sugar Witch gleamed and glowed and slowly slid over to Holden to ask him if he was ready to make a deal.

Out of a long white sleeve, the Sugar Witch pulled out a colorful magic box as she whispered instructions to Holden. The brave knight turned to walk home and the Sugar Witch disappeared.

The box was shiny black with purple stripes, yellow stars, and orange circles. Holden opened up the box and dumped his bag of sweets into it. He left the box in the middle of the kitchen table. He tucked five secret pieces of candy into his armor, glanced out the window into the night, and went upstairs to go to bed.

His armor was heavy as he slipped it off and left it on the foot of his bed. Holden wanted to imagine how the Sugar Witch would swoop down and take the candy, but he fell asleep, sandwiched between his safe, fluffy pillow and his snuggly blanket. He did not dream.

It was the wind and the tree branch hitting Holden's window that woke him up in the morning. Had the Sugar Witch made the switch? Had the whispered trade been done? Holden ran into his kitchen to find the box exactly where he had left it in the middle of the table.

The magic box had overflowed with Halloween treats last night, but they were gone. In the box was a toy knight in shining armor, a toy that Holden had wanted. Holden closed the box and lined the new statue up with some of his other collectible toys. Holden knew he would use the magic box again next Halloween.

Holden never saw the glimmering, white Sugar Witch again in his neighborhood on Halloween night, but each year he left his candy in the black box with purple stripes, yellow stars and orange circles, keeping a few pieces for the next day and each Halloween night the Sugar Witch swooped down to take the candy from the magic box and left Holden a toy.

This year, see if the magic works for you. On Halloween night, place your candy in a colorful box or Halloween bowl, keeping a few secret pieces, and see if the Sugar Witch visits your house and leaves you a toy. Remember the Sugar Witch has become too big to trick or treat and needs your help to create her sugar castle. Be kind like Holden and trade your treats for a great new toy.

 Happy Halloween.

Marcella Ricker is a grandmother who loves reading stories to children, especially those that encourage kindness and healthy habits. She and her family live in Hamilton, Massachusetts.

Harris County Public Library, Houston, TX

CPSIA information can be obtained at www.ICGtesting.com
Printed in the USA
LVOW01s1725300315

432599LV00001B/1/P

9 781480 806924

8